This book belongs to:

....

....

For my lovely little Reuben who makes
any bad day better.

A TEMPLAR BOOK

First published in the UK in 2020 by Templar Books,
an imprint of Bonnier Books UK,
The Plaza, 535 King's Road, London, SW10 0SZ
www.templarco.co.uk
www.bonnierbooks.co.uk

Text and illustrations copyright © 2020 by Frann Preston-Gannon
Design copyright © 2020 by Templar Books
1 3 5 7 9 10 8 6 4 2

ISBN 978-1-78741-565-2 (hardback)
978-1-78741-660-4 (paperback)

This book was typeset in MrsEaves
The illustrations were created with a mixture of ink,
pencils, paints and digital drawing.

Edited by Katie Haworth
Designed by Genevieve Webster
Production by Neil Randles

Printed in China

MIX
Paper from
responsible sources
FSC
www.fsc.org
FSC® C104723

The Bad Day

Frann Preston-Gannon

templar
books

"It's such a lovely morning
and we are pleased to say,
that we can tell it's going to be
a simply **brilliant** day."

"But wait, what's this? I climbed up high
to get this juicy nut.
And now I'm here, it would appear,
I am completely stuck!"

"I thought I'd found some breakfast,
but as you surely see,
things did not go to plan at all;
my face is in a tree."

"My day is also terrible . . .

. . . much worse than what *you've* got.

I tried to swat an irksome fly
and now I'm in a knot!"

"My day is even worse than that,
it's really made me frown.
Everything was going well,
but now I'm upside down!"

"Oh, stop complaining, all of you,
it's more than I can take!
My lunch has disagreed with me
and made my stomach ache."

"The last thing I remember
is a nasty fox's face.
And now it seems that I'm inside
a damp, dark, smelly place!

I really do not like it here.
It's **scary** without doubt.
I want to see the woods again,
please someone . . ."

"Who is that creature in distress?"

"Oh, Mousy, is that you?"

"I think
she's stuck
in Fox's
tum."

"Whatever
will we
do?"

"If we are going to help our friend
we have to act with speed.
I have a nutty plan, my chums,
to get poor Mousy freed!

"If I just swing round on the branch
and use this tail I've got,

the Bird can fly down from the tree . . ."

". . . and help undo Snake's knot."

"Then you two push with all your strength
to flip the Tortoise round . . ."

". . . and if you work together . . .

. . . you can get me to the ground."

"Before we celebrate, my friends,
there's one last thing to do.
I'll use my fluffy tail and then
the Fox will say . . ."

"You animals are wonderful!
Oh, thank you, everyone,
for the brave and daring rescue,
which was scary (but quite fun)!"

"I owe you an apology
for making you my lunch.
I will not eat my friends again,
you're **such** a lovely bunch."

"So when we're feeling gloomy
and in a sorry state,
helping out each other
can make a bad day great!"

The End

Also available:

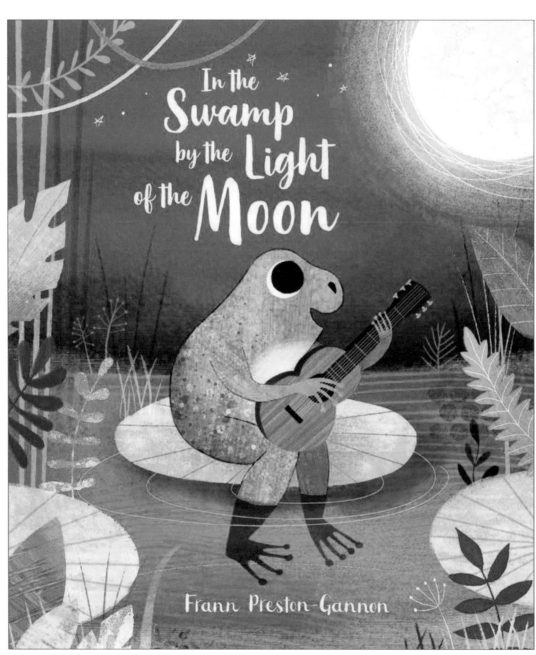

ISBN: 978-1-78741-386-3